Buddy and the Lobster Boat

by **Wendy Graham**

ill   ic

a Capstone company — publishers for children

Engage Literacy is published in the UK by Raintree.
Raintree is an imprint of Capstone Global Library Limited, a company incorporated in England and Wales
having its registered office at 264 Banbury Road, Oxford, OX2 7DY – Registered company number: 6695582

www.raintree.co.uk

Illustration copyright Capstone/Aleksandar Zolotic

Editorial credits
Erika L. Shores, editor; Charmaine Whitman, designer; Katy LaVigne, production specialist

10 9 8 7 6 5 4 3 2 1
Printed and bound in China.

Buddy and the Lobster Boat

ISBN: 978 1 4747 3910 8

Contents

Chapter 1
Buddy comes, too!

Grace loved having a dad who was
a fisherman.
He used his boat to get lobsters from the sea.
On the weekends, Dad often took Grace
out on the lobster boat.
They would check the traps for lobsters.
The traps had bits of chicken in them,
and the lobsters often went into the traps
to eat the chicken.

One morning Grace and Dad were
about to set off on the lobster boat,
when they heard a loud bark.
Grace's dog, Buddy, stood on the beach
wagging his tail.

"Buddy must have followed us," said Grace.
"Can he come, too?"

"No, I think you should take him
back to the house," said Dad.

"Oh, please, Dad," asked Grace.
"Can we bring Buddy?
I'll take care of him."

Buddy jumped around happily.
Dad nodded.
"All right," he smiled.
"Just this once."

Grace grinned as Buddy jumped
into her arms.

Dad started the boat, and it moved away from the jetty.

The first two traps Dad pulled up were empty.
"I really hope we've caught some lobsters in the other traps," said Dad.

Then Dad stopped the boat by the third trap.
"Look!" said Grace.
"You've caught one, Dad!"

Dad checked the lobster to see
if it was big enough to keep.
Because it was large, he placed it
in the big cooler to keep it cold.

Buddy had never seen a lobster before.
He went closer to the open box
for a better look.
The lobster waved its big claws.
Buddy got so scared that he suddenly
jumped back, and over the side he went!

Chapter 2
Buddy's in the water!

"Oh, no!" yelled Grace.

She tried to grab Buddy, but he was
too far away.

He was just out of her reach.

Grace looked into the water.

She could see Buddy between the waves.

"Dad," yelled Grace.

"The waves are too big for him!"

"Grace," said Dad.

"Try to throw the lifebelt over Buddy."

Grace threw the lifebelt but as she did,
the rope dropped into the water.
Another wave pushed Buddy
even farther away.

The boat zoomed across the sea.
Buddy's head bobbed above a large wave.
As Grace watched, Buddy's little legs
paddled as fast as they could.
But he still wasn't close enough
to bring back onto the boat.

Grace had a terrible thought.
What if there were *sharks*!
The thought made her feel sick inside.

From a tiny puppy, Buddy had always
followed Grace everywhere.
But bringing him on the boat trip
had not been a good idea.
Now Buddy was in danger.

Chapter 3
An amazing rescue

"Dad, look!" yelled Grace.
Dad and Grace looked out to sea.
Two dolphins were swimming
on either side of Buddy.
Their fins slid through the water,
as their noses pushed him gently along.

"Dad," said Grace, "the dolphins
are helping Buddy to get to the beach."

When a wave took Buddy away,
the two dolphins pushed him
back towards the beach.

"Amazing!" said Dad.
"Buddy has nearly reached the sand!"
Dad turned the boat towards the beach.

Soon, with a dolphin on each side,
Buddy was washed onto the beach.

Grace jumped from the boat
and grabbed him.
"I've got you, Buddy," she said.

"I can't believe what I just saw!" said Dad.

Grace put Buddy down.
He ran towards the water and barked.

"Buddy knows they saved his life,"
said Grace.
"He is saying thank you to the dolphins!"

Just then, the two dolphins jumped out
of the water before splashing back
into the waves.

Buddy barked again while his tail wagged
up and down.

As if they knew what Buddy was saying,
the dolphins jumped up and then dived
back into the sea.